Walter Hamilton

A memoir of George Cruikshank

Artist and humorist

Walter Hamilton

A memoir of George Cruikshank
Artist and humorist

ISBN/EAN: 9783337118938

Printed in Europe, USA, Canada, Australia, Japan

Cover: Foto ©Raphael Reischuk / pixelio.de

More available books at **www.hansebooks.com**

A MEMOIR

OF

GEORGE CRUIKSHANK,

Artist and Humourist.

WITH NUMEROUS ILLUSTRATIONS,

AND A

£1 BANK NOTE.

BY

WALTER HAMILTON, F.R.G.S.

London:

ELLIOT STOCK, 62, PATERNOSTER ROW, E.C.

1878.

A SHORT time before the death of the late lamented GEORGE CRUIKSHANK, I read a lecture on his works before the Chelsea Literary and Scientific Institution.

With a few slight additions that lecture is now presented to the public.

Unfortunately, however, the hundreds of rare and splendid examples of the artist's genius which illustrated that lecture cannot be reproduced.

We may hope that the autobiography upon which the artist had long been at work, and which cannot fail to be interesting, will ere long be published. In the meantime this little tribute to his memory, from one who was honoured with his friendship, may be interesting to collectors of his works, and of some use in drawing attention to the beauties they contain.

WALTER HAMILTON.

DUKE ST., ADELPHI,
February, 1878.

GEORGE CRUIKSHANK.

CONSIDERED simply as an artist and etcher, CRUIKSHANK was one of the most remarkable men of the nineteenth century; but when we survey the incidents of his long and industrious life, we find in it so much to amuse, instruct, and elevate, that we know not where to turn for his equal, either in this century, or in times gone by.

As a political caricaturist, as an original humourist, as the illustrator of other men's works, either in history, poetry, or fiction, and finally as the stern exposer of abuses, and the faithful advocate of Temperance principles, the number and variety of his drawings are unparalleled by those of any of his predecessors or contemporaries. His characteristic signature is to be found at the foot of thousands of pictures full of merriment or drollery; sometimes pathetic, often weird; now quaintly imaginative, or poetically ideal; at other times terrible to a startling extent (*teste* " Fagin in the Condemned Cell"); often full of wonderfully accurate architectural detail, or archæological study of buildings and costume. From the fanciful illustrations of *The Life of Sir John Falstaff*, turn to the vivid, realistic scenes in *The Irish Rebellion*, and then to the wonderfully accurate anatomical drawings which accompany Dr. Pettigrew's celebrated medical work on *The History of Egyptian Mummies* (published forty-four years ago),

B

one scarcely knows in which line to say he excels, so marvellous was his versatility.

In what other artist can we find such a combination of talents, or so great a variety in excellence? Not in Goya or Callot, Holbein or Rembrandt; not in Hogarth, Rowlandson, or Gilray, still less in Gavarni, Seymour, Leech, or Tenniel. The elder, Isaac Cruikshank, and Robert the brother of George, resemble him in some of their works, but, taken as a whole, have far less merit than he.

It is decidedly unfair to CRUIKSHANK to rank him simply as a caricaturist, but it is in this particular branch of art that his works come most easily in comparison with those of other artists. Space will not permit me to write at length on the interesting subject of Caricatures. It must, therefore, suffice to mention the titles of a few works, to which reference may easily be made by any one desirous of following up the history of Caricature:—*L'Histoire de la Caricature, Antique, Moyen Age, et Moderne*, (3 vols.; Champfleury, Paris); *The Life of Gilray* (T. Wright); *History of Caricature, and of the Grotesque in Art* (T. Wright); *Caricature History of the Four Georges* (T. Wright); also a few papers in the *Leisure Hour* for 1875, containing a brief *résumé* of the principal English Caricaturists.

The leaders may be here referred to. They are—

William Hogarth (1697—1764). The father of English caricature, and, probably, the *wittiest* man on canvas the world has produced. Any enumeration of his works is, of course, unnecessary. As the fearless exposer of social and moral abuses, he takes the first rank. Mr. Sala's articles on Hogarth, which appeared in the first volume of *The Cornhill Magazine*, contain an excellent account of the artist and his works.

T. Rowlandson (1756—1827). The works of this

artist are coarse, and no great interest is now attached
to them, beyond a comparatively small circle of collectors. The public are principally acquainted with
him through his illustrations to the various tours of
Dr. Syntax. His principal defect is the gross exaggeration of female figures, which are usually ugly and
coarse to a disgusting degree.

Isaac Cruikshank was a political caricaturist, con-
temporary with Rowlandson. He was a follower of
Pitt, whom he represents in one of his pieces as the
Royal extinguisher putting out the flame of sedition.
In addition to these more important works, he seems to
have done an immense number of small cuts for cheap
editions of plays, children's books, etc. These illustrations are, however, destitute of any merit. The
father of Robert and GEORGE CRUIKSHANK, he imparted
to them a certain amount of technical instruction and
art training, and in his later works was much assisted
by their co-operation.

J. Gilray (1785—1815). A political caricaturist,
and, as an artist, greatly superior to Rowlandson. His
best works are those in which he ridicules the weak-
nesses and parsimony of George III., and his by no
means amiable Queen. He also published many bitter
satires directed against the Great Napoleon and his
Court, and did as much as lay in his power to keep up
the war fever under which our forefathers were then
labouring. Most of these works have been beautifully
reproduced in the *Life of Gilray*, by T. Wright, a most
useful guide to the history of the times. The political
series of his caricatures commences in the year 1782,
shortly before the coalition between Fox and Lord
North, and continues until 1810. It comprises not less
than four hundred plates, giving an average of about
fourteen for each year. Sir Francis Burdett was a pro-

minent figure in many of Gilray's latest caricatures in
the year 1809. One of the earliest of GEORGE CRUIK-
SHANK'S works represents the arrest of the Baronet
under the warrant of the Speaker, in 1810. The series
is thus taken up without the omission of a single link
in the consecutive caricature history of the period.

Robert Cruikshank, who died in 1856, has left many

specimens of his genius, such as *Monsieur Nontongpaw,
The Devil's Walk, Thomas's Burlesque Dramas, Monsieur Mallet*, etc., etc.   In many of these works the fancy
seems as bright, and the execution as successful, as
in those of his brother George.   Fortunately I am
enabled to present my readers with several very

characteristic examples of his work. In some of the
earlier works of Robert Cruikshank there was an
evident imitation of Bewick's style, as will be seen
from the first half-dozen illustrations. Later on
we come to some humorous sketches, such as the
"Monkey running away with the Old Maid's spectacles," "Dustmen Carousing," "The Philosopher so

rapt in Study that he does not notice the Cat chasing the Parrot," and "The Wandering Musicians." But the best of all, "King Death Pursuing the Tailor"

and "The Monkey Taking Physic," are worthy of his
brother for humourous conception, although the execution is rough to the last degree.

This brother left a son, Percy Cruikshank, also an artist, and an unscrupulous publisher made use of that name in a way to merit the following rebuke, prefixed to each part of the *Fairy Library* :—

"To the Public.

"I think it a duty to inform the public that I have a nephew whose Christian name is PERCY. He is employed by a person of the name of READ, a publisher, of Johnson's Court, Fleet Street, who, in advertising any work executed by my nephew, announces it as by *Cruikshank*, instead of as illustrated by Percy Cruikshank. I hereby caution the public against buying any work as mine with the name of Mr. READ, of Johnson's Court, upon it as publisher. *I never did anything for that person, and never shall.*

"GEORGE CRUIKSHANK."

Robert Seymour.—Amongst more modern artists we first come to the name of poor Robert Seymour, who committed suicide in 1836. This clever young artist devoted his rare talents almost exclusively to ridiculing the vagaries of cockney sportsmen, occasionally indulging in harmless satire at the expense of dustmen and costermongers. He commenced to illustrate the *Pickwick Papers*. On his death, Mr. Thackeray, then an unknown man, applied for the vacant post; but, fortunately, Dickens declined his request. I say *fortunately*, for Thackeray's pen was a more valuable instrument than his pencil.

Mat Morgan, a scene painter by profession, will be chiefly remembered from his connection with the defunct *Tomahawk.* His cartoons were remarkable for great force, much originality, and the extraordinary effects of light and shade they contained. In one respect his work resembled that of John Tenniel, the draughtsman of the *Punch* cartoons, namely, that the political personages are only very slightly caricatured in feature or person, the principal humour consisting in representing dignified statesmen in some homely or menial capacity having some degree of fancied similarity to the political circumstance of the moment. In this particular line, Mat Morgan's creations possess much greater originality than those of Tenniel. The weekly cartoons of the latter artist may be said to be pictorial representations of the leading articles of the *Times*. Tenniel is seldom witty, and only occasionally humourous, but he can be very pathetic, and is by far the most correct *artist* employed on the periodical press.

John Leech (1817—1864) was for many years the most valued, and most amusing contributor to *Punch*. He is the only modern artist whose name and fame come at all near those of our hero, and he, in one respect, was decidedly superior to GEORGE CRUIKSHANK, namely, in his female characters.

Leech drew lovely women and pretty children, not such lackadaisical drawing room fine ladies as Du Maurier reproduces week after week with tiresome repetition, but real live, jolly girls, with plenty of fun and mischief; and happy, romping children, drawn from the people and for the people.

Du Maurier's ladies are all of one type, they are all absurdly tall, and they and the children are almost invariably dressed in the height of the fashion, as though there were no people in England but the class vulgarly called the *Upper Ten*, who monopolised all the mirth and pleasantry to be found in this country. There is a snobbishness about this artist's work exceedingly inconsistent with anything like genuine humour, and it is refreshing to turn back to earlier numbers of *Punch* to see the pretty girls, the happy lovers, the cosy married couples, and deliciously mischievous children of Leech. Now CRUIKSHANK does not deal with the *pretty*, and even in his illustrations to novels it is comparatively seldom that we meet with a comely woman. Making all allowances for the curious changes in the fashions of ladies' dress, which the dear old artist had to portray during his career, it will be found that his ladies are chiefly remarkable for having very small, wasplike waists, tiny feet and ancles, large faces with high foreheads, aquiline noses, very piercing eyes, and a profusion of short ringlets. It is no exaggeration to say that many of his ladies have waists decidedly smaller round than their necks, a very curious anatomical blunder for such an artist to make. Of course, there are exceptions, notably in the fairy tale books, where the girls and little children are ravishingly beautiful, and as full of grace and sweetness as can be found in lovely nature itself.

Thackeray, too, having been educated as an artist, took a delight in illustrating his own novels and tales; and very queer and quaint and funny many of his pictures are, and very useful in conveying his meaning; but they are uncouth, unfinished, and decidedly inferior to those of CRUIKSHANK. As an artist, Thackeray had little success; but having tried to become one, he knew the difficulties that lay in the way of a struggling aspirant to fame, and was patient and considerate when criticising the work of other men. Fortunately, he found in literature more encouragement than in art; yet he always retained his love for art, and his writings contain some of the finest criticisms in the language. He especially delighted in CRUIKSHANK, and the celebrated article he wrote for the *Westminster Review* is replete with kindly encouragement and earnest praise, mingled with much characteristic pathos and humour. This article did much towards directing public attention to CRUIKSHANK'S works, and, being illustrated with well-selected specimens, it had a large sale. The printer to the magazine thereupon produced a number of surreptitious copies which he had printed for his own use, and these also had a large sale. A copy of the article, in good preservation, and with all the illustrations, is now considered cheap at twenty times its original price. It must be remembered also that Thackeray wrote a very appreciative and interesting *critique* on the works of Leech.

In addition to these well-known names there are many others of considerable merit, such as "H. B." (Mr. Doyle); Hablot K. Brown, known as "Phiz;" A. H. Forrester, known as "Alfred Crowquill" and "Onwynn."

GEORGE CRUIKSHANK was born in London on 27th September, 1792, and died at his house in the Hampstead Road, at about half-past seven o'clock on the 1st of February, 1878. He was therefore more than eighty-five years of age, and so industrious has he always been that the amount of his work is almost inconceivable. Some idea of its extent may be gained from the splendid Catalogue of his works, published by Bell and Daldy, in three volumes, in which mention is made of 5,080 separate productions, and that list is known to be incomplete; besides which it only comes down to the year 1870: since that time he has done some excellent work. In the Westminster Aquarium are some sketches executed by him seventy-seven years ago, and he illustrated *The Rose and the Lily*, only last year, with one of the prettiest etchings he ever did. Whilst the great Catalogue was being prepared by Mr. Reid, he wrote the following interesting letter to that gentleman :—

GEORGE CRUIKSHANK TO MR. REID.

"DEAR SIR,—In the compiling of such a list as this, it is not at all surprising that there should be errors, particularly when we look at the fact of their being three in one family (a father and two sons), all working in similar styles, and upon the same sort of subjects. My father, *Isaac Cruikshank*, was a designer and etcher, and engraver, and a first-rate water-colour draughtsman. My brother, *Isaac Robert*, was a very clever miniature and portrait painter, and was also a designer and etcher; and your humble servant likewise a designer and etcher.

"When I was a mere boy, my dear father kindly allowed me to *play* at *etching* on some of his copper plates—little bits of shadows, or little figures in the background—and to assist him a *little* as I grew older ; and he used to assist *me* in putting in hands and faces. And when my dear brother *Robert* (who in his latter days omitted the *Isaac*) left off portrait painting and took almost entirely to designing and etching, I assisted him at first to a great extent in some of his drawings on wood and his etchings ; and all this mixture of head and hand work has led to a considerable amount of confusion, so that dealers or printsellers and collectors have been puzzled to decide which were the productions of the ' I. CK.,' the ' I. R. CK.' (or ' R. CK.'), and the 'G. CK.'; and this will not create much surprise when I tell you that I have myself, in some cases had a difficulty in deciding in respect to early *hand-work*, done some sixty odd years back, particularly when my drawings, made on wood blocks for common purposes, were hastily executed (according to price) by the engraver. Many of my first productions, such as halfpenny lottery pictures and books for little children, can never be known or seen, having, of course, been destroyed long ago by the dear little ones who had them to play with.

"I may just add that my brother, ' I. R. C.,' left a son, whose name is Percy, who is a draughtsman and wood engraver, and has a son, whose name is George, also an artist. As the *two Georges* create confusion, he intends, I believe, in future, to add his mother's family name to his own, and sign himself ' *George Calvert* Cruikshank,' or take his father's Christian name of Percy.

"In conclusion, I think I may safely say you will now place before the public a perfect catalogue—at least, one which is as near perfect as possible—of all the marks made on *paper, wood, copper*, or *steel*, by the hand of   "Yours truly,

"263, Hampstead Road,   "GEORGE CRUIKSHANK.
    "*February* 15, 1870."

———

A writer in the *Daily Telegraph* justly observed that as a manipulator of copper and steel GEORGE CRUIK-SHANK may be held to be the foremost representative of an art which, to most illustrative intents and pur-poses, is as defunct as lithography.

Photography utterly slew the art of drawing on stone—that is, in black and white. Chromo-lithography yet lives, and will continue to be largely turned to decorative use. But illustrative etching has been wholly beaten out of the field by wood engraving.

When CRUIKSHANK was in his prime, copper was the

only material used for etching, and an impression of two, or, at the most, three thousand, wore a plate completely out The artist tells us himself that in consequence of the prodigious demand for his celebrated etching of "Jack Ketch's Promissory Note" (a Bank Note not to be imitated) he was obliged to sit up a whole night to engrave a second plate, the first one being exhausted. And when Thackeray projected the *Cornhill Magazine*, he found to his great disappointment that a circulation of 80,000 copies would not permit of the illustrations being printed apart from the type, and he was compelled to abandon his favourite copper and steel plates for the rough-and-ready wood blocks. It was evident, therefore, that in the face of such obstacles the art of illustrative etching must necessarily decline.

Apart from CRUIKSHANK'S merits as an etcher, he has attained distinguished success as a draughtsman on wood, in which branch of art his works are regarded as the most beautiful examples extant, and have earned for him the enthusiastic praise of so severe a critic as John Ruskin.

CRUIKSHANK was of Scotch descent, and his ancestors were involved in the '45 rebellion, but he himself was a thorough Englishman in his tastes, his prejudices, and his conceptions. His domestic pictures display an English love for home and its comforts, good living, bright fires, and cheerful faces. His outdoor scenery is often conventional, but always English, the meadows studded with trees, the summer sky toned down with swiftly passing fleecy clouds, the hedges and ditches, and the country people are all thoroughly English.

When he had to draw a Frenchman, he produced the regular old type of Frenchman, with spindle-shanks, shrugging shoulders, and outstretched hands. It must be confessed that for that great nation Mr. CRUIKSHANK entertained considerable contempt. He had quite the

ante-steam days British idea of a Frenchman; and if
he did not believe that the inhabitants of France were
for the most part dancing-masters and barbers, yet he
took care to depict such in preference, and would not
speak too well of them.

Robert, his elder brother by exactly three years, was
a sailor, for which life George also had a great taste,
and it is very noticeable what a decided liking both of
them showed in early life for depicting scenes of naval
life, and how admirably they caught the spirit and gaiety
of our Jack Tars. Amongst the earliest efforts of George
were small cuts of ships to show the different styles of
rigging, and in the more ambitious works, such as
Greenwich Hospital, *Dibdin's Sea Songs*, and *The Old
Sailor's Jolly Boat*, the accuracy and force with which
ships, sea, and seamen are drawn is marvellous, and
will form a useful guide to future generations of the
appearance of our Navy before the days of steam and
ironclads.

His career as an artist commenced more than seventy
years ago, in the days when the sallow-faced General
Buonaparte was First Consul of the French Republic,
and amongst his early works are caricatures of that
wonderful man, then so much dreaded in this country.
Those were quite the " dark ages," in more senses than
one, for gas was not yet in use, as we can see from
many an old London street scene then drawn by GEORGE
CRUIKSHANK. In fact, a complete collection of his
works would give an intelligent foreigner a more clear
and vivid impression of the politics, costume, amuse-
ments, literature, and popular prejudices of the English
people for the last three-quarters of a century, than any
history I have ever met with. He caricatured Napoleon,
and he illustrated a life of him; he ridiculed, in a harmless sort of way, poor old George III.; and then he
satirised the detestable George IV. as bitterly as he
deserved.

When tea was eight or ten shillings a pound, he praised it; and was quite of a contrary opinion to Tom Hood, who tells us that—

> "If wine is a poison, so is tea,
> Though in another shape;
> What matter whether one is killed
> By *canister* or *grape*?"

When he was a young man, beer was the common beverage for breakfast, for tea was an expensive luxury. In his young days it was a very common event to hang half-a-dozen people in one morning at the Old Bailey, for very slight crimes; whilst now people have, and rightly, a very decided dislike to capital punishment, under any circumstances.

In his early days, stage coaches were the modes of conveyance. Now, conveyancing is done either by the railway companies or the solicitors, and coaches are extinct, except in a few University cities, where they are employed by young gentlemen whose brains require a few more inside passengers in the shape of dates, facts, and the chaste incidents in the lives of the gods and goddesses of ancient classical mythology, which are found so useful in after-life. But, speaking of mythology, there is one branch of it on which CRUIK-SHANK is an undoubted authority. But for his genius, we never should have known anything of Fairy Mythology, whilst now we know quite as much as the fairies themselves—perhaps more. And in one great feature his works on the subject are preferable to any of the Classical Mythologies. CRUIKSHANK is pure and innocent;—no need to lock up his works, whatever may be the topic. This much cannot certainly be said of Dr. Lemprière's deities.

Old or young or middle aged can understand and appreciate CRUIKSHANK. Each age, perhaps, may take a different stand-point for admiration, but the admiration will be unanimous.

More than sixty years since, G. CRUIKSHANK was a

C

private in the Loyal North British Volunteers, and again came forward, in 1859, to take part in the modern and—it is to be hoped—permanent Volunteer force then organised, when he became the Lieutenant-Colonel of his corps, the Havelock Volunteers. But it will be impossible to enumerate all the curious historical events which have transpired during his lifetime, and with many of which he has been artistically connected, from the invention of lucifer matches and penny ices, to the creation of the vast railway system of England and the new police. He illustrated all the best works of our early novelists, and was celebrated in that capacity before Dickens, Thackeray, Albert Smith, or Bulwer Lytton were born ; yet he afterwards knew them as men, and outlived them all. Suffice it to say, that until the last few weeks he was living amongst us, a hearty, handsome, kindly old gentleman, who could sing a good song, make a good speech, or tell a good tale with any one. He had been happy in his work, and had made millions happy with it. He was loved by all who knew him, and by millions who knew him only by his works.

England had made rapid strides in education, culture, comfort, and sobriety during his lifetime, and he was hopeful it would continue still to do so. In only one direction was he fearful for the future. *Intemperance* keeps the people back, or, at least, a portion of it ; and it must be admitted that no man has worked harder in the *Total Abstinence* movement than the artist who drew " The Bottle," " The Drunkard's Children," and " The Worship of Bacchus."

The following are his own words on the subject. Speaking at the Field Lane Institution in 1876, he remarked that a very great mistake was made about temperance and teetotalism. " If (he said) intoxicating liquor could be taken without danger, then temperance would be a good principle ; but as it was a deadly poison and did so much mischief, the best thing was to abstain from it altogether; therefore, he maintained that total abstinence should be the rule. He had been working for many years to try and stop the use of these drinks, but he could not succeed. When he brought out *The Bottle*, he was not a total abstainer. The scenes from *The Bottle* were represented at many theatres, one or two of which he visited to see how the audiences took his *Bottle*. Although they appeared impressed with the tragic incidents represented, yet they all went out and had something to drink. At last he found it was no use preaching without setting an example; therefore he became a total abstainer, and had been one for the last thirty years. He used also to smoke, but was glad to say that he had now left off that bad habit."

From these remarks it will be seen how stern and uncompromising his views were. We may not all agree with his conclusions, but we must at least admire his sincerity and self-denial. He was consistent, and practised what he preached.

Englishmen who have travelled abroad have learnt that in foreign countries, where wines and spirits are very cheap and very good, temperance, not total abstinence, is the rule; and that a drunken man and a tee-totaller are equally rare. And even in England, intemperance is now almost confined to one class, for it is certainly no longer considered a gentlemanly accomplishment to get intoxicated, as it was in the time of the Georges.

Let us remember that for the poorer classes the public house is the only place which offers warmth, light, and some degree of comfort during the long dreary winter evenings, and that many frequent it, not so much for the drink they are almost compelled to consume, as for the lack of home comforts and cheerful recreation. On Sundays there is nowhere else to go, as all innocent and instructive places of resort are closed on that day, and there is absolutely no choice between the church and the tavern, for when one shuts the other opens. If every one went to church even three times on Sunday, there would still remain a long time unoccupied, during which the hated beer shops would do a large business in the sale of the vile, because adulterated, liquors which debases the intellect and ruins the health of those who consume them.

Educate and elevate the people, give them books to read, let them have innocent recreation on Sundays, and open the museums more freely on that day than any other, encourage them to have comfortable homes, and drunkenness will die out of itself.

Unfortunately Mr. CRUIKSHANK has left no children to inherit his genius and imitate his virtues. He was twice married; and on the 8th March, 1875, he celebrated what is called *The Silver Wedding*, on which occasion the author had the good fortune to be one of the many friends present, to wish the veteran artist and his amiable wife long life and happiness.

To receive the congratulations of so many friends was a task which would have fatigued and excited many a younger man than Mr. CRUIKSHANK; but he preserved his self-possession through it well, having a ready jest and a smile for each and all, whilst Mrs. Cruikshank, who was fairly hedged in on every side with bouquets, looked far too young to be one of the principals in such a ceremony. A guard of honour from his old *corps* attended to do honour to their late Colonel. It was late in the afternoon before Mr. CRUIKSHANK withdrew for a few moments from the crowded rooms, and as he went he whispered, laughingly, to the author, "You are down on our list of visitors for the Golden Wedding."

It was proposed to present a public testimonial to Mr. CRUIKSHANK on the occasion of the "Silver

Wedding;" but this honour he declined, and the only event of importance in his recent career was the purchase by the Westminster Aquarium of a large and extremely interesting collection of his paintings, engravings, and original sketches, to which every admirer of humour and artistic skill should pay a visit, and carefully study the works. Many are so crowded with figures and details that time is required to discover all their beauties, and it is best to go when in a laughing mood. A dull or serious state of mind is fatal to a full appreciation of CRUIKSHANK.

" There must be no smiling with Cruikshank. A man who does not laugh outright is a dullard, and has no heart. Even the old ' Dandy of Sixty ' (George IV.) must have laughed at his own wondrous grotesque image, as they say Louis Philippe did, who saw all the caricatures that were made of himself. And there are some of Cruikshank's designs which have the blessed faculty of creating laughter as often as you see them."

It is in fairy scenes that the delicacy of touch, the exquisite finish, and above all the really poetical imagination of CRUIKSHANK are displayed to the fullest extent. His ghosts and his fairies are exactly like what we imagine such beings must appear. When the numbers of tiny faces, full of expression, are carefully examined, it will be seen that every feature is drawn, even in a face the size of a pin's head, and drawn with many strokes; indeed, the simplest illustration must consist of thousands of little lines slowly and laboriously scratched on copper with an etching needle. In his small animals the same extraordinary finish is to be found (see, for instance, the rats in the frontispiece to *The Pentamerone*, or the geese opposite page 298). Per·haps, however, the most charming instance of all, is the little plate in *Grimm's Tales*, of the elves putting on their nether garments.

For tragical power, his illustrations in Maxwell's *Irish Rebellion* are very remarkable, tinged though they are with a keen insight into the drollery and dare-devil character of those poor natives of beautiful Erin, of whom the poet so touchingly remarks :—

" For dear is the Emerald Isle of the Ocean,
   Whose daughters are fair as the foam of the wave ;
   Whose sons, unaccustom'd to rebel commotion,
   Tho' joyous, are sober—tho' peaceful, are brave."

In his *Elements of Drawing*, Ruskin says—" His tragic power, though rarely developed, and warped by habits of caricature, is, in reality, as great as his grotesque power."

If we do not find the brilliant antithesis of ideas which characterises the wit of Hogarth, in such a picture as " The Wedding in Marylebone Church," where the cobweb is shown over the lid of the poor-box ; nor such wit as is seen in the intensely comical, but execrably ill-drawn punning sketches of Tom Hood, there is yet an expression of drollery in the faces and attitudes of his characters which appeals quite as strongly to our risibility. Where, for instance, could the equal be found, for humour in drawing, to the sketch of the marine saluting his officer, and complaining, " Please yer honour, Tom Towzer's tied my tail so tight that I cannot shut my eyes." The stiff attitude of poor Joey the marine, with his pigtail sticking out straight behind him, and the skin of his face drawn tightly back over his ears, is inexpressibly laughable. Or, again, examine that comical little cut of the vain dog who curled his tail so tightly that it lifted him off his hind legs.

— " The Tutors Assistant —

With pardonable pride CRUIKSHANK refers to the
success of some of his endeavours, in the preface to the
Catalogue of the Exhibition of his works at the Westminster Aquarium.

This collection, containing works produced between
1799—1875, shows the efforts he made to improve the
customs of society. The works of 1799, mentioned in
the title of this catalogue, were, of course, the works of
a very little boy, and were only exhibited as curiosities ;
but in the early years of the present century, GEORGE
CRUIKSHANK began etching for the printsellers as a
means of living. He drew Lord Nelson's funeral car
in 1805, and made some illustrations of the O. P. Riots
at Covent Garden Theatre in 1809. To glance over the
Catalogue recalls a number of names that now seem
almost antediluvian, though in CRUIKSHANK'S youth
they were the living centres of interest, great and
small. Bonaparte (under his popular nickname of
" Boney "), Alderman Curtis, the elder Mathews,
the comedian Liston, Sir Francis Burdett, Cobbett,
" Orator " Hunt, Wooler (the editor of a publication
called the *Black Dwarf*), Carlile the publisher, William
Hone, Major Cartwright, Sir John Cam Hobhouse,
the Cato Street conspirators, and other celebrities
of Prince Regent and George IV. days—these are the
persons we find depicted in the early sketches of
CRUIKSHANK.

His first designs were in connection with cheap songs
and children's books. Then he furnished political caricatures to the *Scourge*, and some other satirical publications, and did a good deal of work for Mr. Hone's
books and periodicals, during several years. Some
special hits were made in connection with the trial of
Queen Caroline, a subject on which the public mind
was greatly excited. One of these designs, called " The
Queen's Matrimonial Ladder," ran through about fifty
editions. It was accompanied by a small " Toy," now

exceedingly scarce, of which the following is a *fac
simile* :—

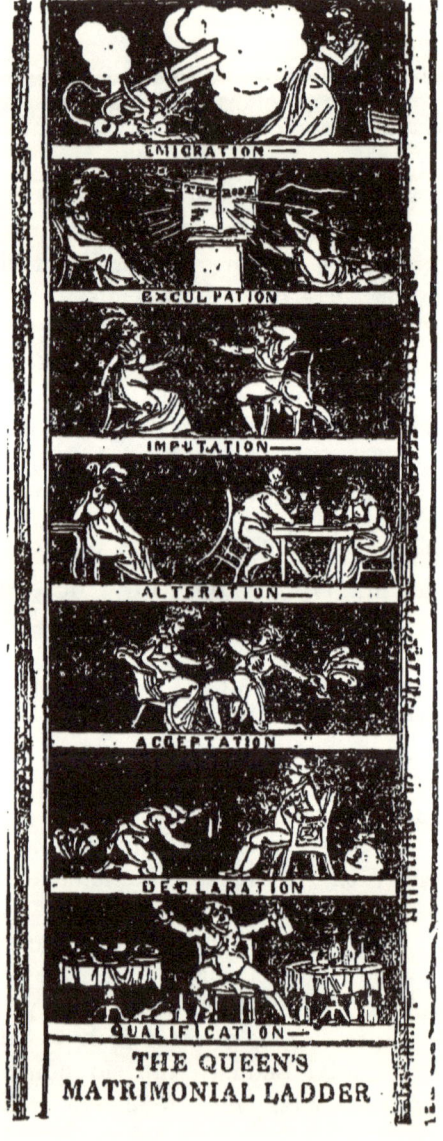

THE QUEEN'S
MATRIMONIAL LADDER

REMIGRATION

CONSTERNATION

ACCUSATION

PUBLICATION

INDIGNATION

CORONATION

DEGRADATION

PRINTED BY WILLIAM HONE,
LUDGATE HILL, LONDON;
Price (with the Pamphlet) One Shilling.

Other caricatures, bearing the titles "Non Mi Ricordo," "The Political House that Jack Built,"

THE DANDY OF SIXTY.

" This is THE MAN—all shaven and shorn,
All cover'd with orders—and all forlorn ;
THE DANDY OF SIXTY,
  who bows with a grace,
And has *taste* in wigs, collars,
   cuirasses and lace ;
Who, to tricksters and fools,
   leaves the State and its treasure,
And, when Britain's in tears,
   sails about at his pleasure :
Who spurn'd from his presence
   the Friends of his youth,
And now has not one
   who will tell him the truth ;
Who took to his counsels,
   in evil hour,
The Friends to the Reasons
   of lawless Power ;
That back the Public Informer,
   who
Would put down the *Thing*,
   that, in spite of new Acts,
And attempts to restrain it,
   by Soldiers or Tax,
Will *poison* the Vermin,
That plunder the Wealth,
That lay in the House,
That Jack built."

" The Political Showman," and " A Slap at Slop ; or, the Bridge Street Gang," likewise attained great success ;

and it is said that altogether Hone made nearly a thousand pounds by these prints, though the artist received only half a guinea each for them.

Irrespective of any party feeling, it is now admitted that Hone's political tracts were almost entirely destitute of any *literary* merit. They sold in enormous numbers, partly because Hone espoused the popular cause, but principally, no doubt, on account of the clever illustrations.

Hone has been accused of meanness towards the artist; yet he probably paid him more than others would have done, and, being engaged in a very dangerous business, he took all responsibility on himself. No slight risk; for it must be remembered that the Government frequently prosecuted him for various publications, and Hone never was at any time a rich man. Hone was at least a man of his word; he paid CRUIKSHANK what he agreed to pay, for he well knew how true was the advice that an opposing critic tendered him : --

"Make much of that droll dog, and feed him fat ;
Your gains would fall off sadly in amount,
Should he once think your letterpress too flat,
And take to writing on his own account :
Your libels then would sell about as quick, sir,
As bare quack labels would without th'elixir."

GEORGE CRUIKSHANK, as an artist, possessed genius of the highest order. Thoroughly original, he created a style for himself, and made it popular. What he thus initiated he completed, for no one has followed in his steps with any success. He has no equal; he has no rival; he created his school, and it will die with him. He could give an appearance of vitality to even the most inanimate objects. Half a lemon, or a pair of spectacles, or a pot of beer, an oyster or a mushroom, can be found full of life and expression in *Three Courses and a Dessert*, a little work which contains some of his finest woodcuts. Look, too, at the four charming etchings in *The Bee and*

the Wasp; in the third plate, the attitude and expression
given to the wasp, who is sneering at the bee, after
having beguiled him into the honey-pot, are as fiendish
as it is possible to conceive, though the personality of
the wasp is fully preserved.

Plate No. 2, where the bee and the wasp are gaily
carousing together, is nearly as fine ; the graceful form
of the wasp, and his features of the Mephistophelean
type, contrast well with the stout, sober, middle-aged,
respectable appearance of poor Mr. Humble Bee.

Plus philosophe qu'on ne pense! a Belgian artist wittily
wrote under a picture of two lovers kissing. Does not
this remark aptly characterise the whole of CRUIK-
SHANK'S labours ? Seldom destitute of a moral, over-
flowing with animal spirits and good humour, there is
nothing in all the gems of English literature to vie
with his productions for innocent mirth, and insight
into modern social life and character.

No one who has paid the slightest attention to the
works of CRUIKSHANK will have failed to perceive that
in all his works, whether comic or serious, there has
been an undercurrent of moral teaching, varying in
intensity as in subject.

Cruelty, tyranny, ignorance, folly, crime, and intemperance have never been more powerfully, or more
clearly denounced in pulpit or court than in the works
of this artist.

The vile orgies which took place at the "St. Bar-
tholomew Fair" were so exposed in the "Fiend's
Frying Pan" that that fair was abolished, to be followed
shortly afterwards by Greenwich Fair, only one degree
less vicious. The most striking instance of his power
as a reformer is to be found in the history of his
"Bank Note *not* to be Imitated." This is his account
of the origin of that singular work :—

"Fifty-eight years back from this date (1876), there were ' one
pound ' Bank of England notes in circulation, and, unfortunately,

many forged notes were in circulation also, or being 'passed,' the punishment for which offence was in some cases transportation, in others DEATH. At this period, having to go early one morning to the Royal Exchange, I passed Newgate jail and saw several persons suspended from the gibbet, *two* of these were women who had been executed for passing *one pound* forged notes.

" I determined if possible to put a stop to such a terrible punishment for such a crime, and made a sketch of the above note, and then an etching of it.

" Mr. Hone published it, and it created a *sensation*. The Directors of the Bank of England were exceedingly wrath. The crowd round Hone's shop in Ludgate Hill was so great that the Lord Mayor had to send the police to clear the street. The notes were in such demand that they could not be printed fast enough, and I had to sit up all one night to etch another plate. Mr. Hone realised above £700, and I had the satisfaction of knowing that no man or woman was ever hanged after this for passing one-pound forged Bank of England notes.

" The issue of my ' Bank Note *not* to be Imitated ' not only put a stop to the issue of any more Bank of England one pound notes, but also put a stop to the punishment of death for such an offence— not only for that, but likewise for forgery—and then the late Sir Robert Peel revised the Penal Code ; so that the final effect of *my note* was to stop the hanging for all minor offences, and has thus been the means of saving thousands of men and women from being hanged."

Last, but most important of all, his efforts in the cause of Temperance have been many and powerful. A consistent total abstainer himself (since 1847), he waged war against the consumption of any intoxicating drink. It is a war of extermination ; he gives *no quarter ;* he will grant no concession. To stay the drunkenness of the few, he sees no other means than to deprive the temperate many. All sensible people deplore the lamentable extent of intemperance in England, but comparatively few believe that the means employed by Temperance societies are fitted to attain the end at which they aim.

Anything more humorous than the sketches of drunken men to be found in his early works can scarcely be imagined, nothing more terrible than his later exposures of the evils of drink have ever been drawn.

The two well-known series, " The Bottle " and " The Drunkard's Children," created much sensation when they appeared, and dramas were written up to the pictures, and performed at several theatres.

His large oil-painting, entitled " The Worship of Bacchus ; or, the Drinking Customs of Society," is too well known to require any comment. It was purchased by subscription, and presented to the nation. It has also been engraved, and large numbers have been sold.

Besides these large works, numbers of Temperance tracts, tales, and sheets have been illustrated by him, and, on that account principally, have sold so well, that most of them are out of print, and nearly all are scarce.

The connection between G. CRUIKSHANK and the Temperance party was a long and honourable one, for although we may not all choose to take the pledge, some good has been effected through the exertions of Temperance societies, and the genius of the great artist was never more usefully or more successfully applied than in depicting the horrors of drunkenness, and the evils it entails not only on the poor degraded drunkard himself, but upon every one connected with him. At the same time, no artist has ever more humourously depicted the comical side of this question, for it has its comic phases, and his drunken people are unmistakeably so, when he only wishes to show that side of the question. Indeed, until quite of late years, it would seem that, with all his hatred for the vice, he could only with great difficulty ignore its comic aspects.

It was in connection with the Temperance question that a curious controversy arose between Charles Dickens and the artist, which appears to have led to a coolness between them, never entirely removed. G. CRUIKSHANK illustrated the four very old fairy tales, *Jack and the Beanstalk, Hop-o'-my-Thumb, Cinderella,* and *Puss in Boots;* and the etchings rank amongst his finest works. These books were intended for the use and amusement of children; but finding that the old editions contained much that was indecent, cruel, and altogether unsuited for children, Mr. CRUIKSHANK altered some parts of the tales, with a view of making them the vehicles of moral instruction and Temperance principles.

Dickens thereupon published a paper in *Household Words,* entitled "Frauds upon the Fairies," in which the alterations made by the artist were most severely criticised, chiefly on the score that he has made these tales the means of conveying his own opinions to the world.

Mr. CRUIKSHANK'S reply to this article consists of an enumeration of the many objectionable passages he had felt it necessary to remove or to alter, and asserts the undoubted right an author has to remodel the work of a bygone age to suit his purpose, and more particularly so, if that purpose be an admittedly good one. In conclusion, he points out that the early editions of these tales differ materially one from another. This unfortunate disagreement was evidently very painful for the artist, as it could scarcely fail to be from the intemperate tone of the criticism. In the earliest printed replies CRUIKSHANK refers to the mistake "*my friend* Charles Dickens has fallen into;" in later copies "my friend" gives way to the formal *Mr.* Charles Dickens.

Dickens, who knew as well as any man in England the terrible curse that drunkenness is to his country, has so clearly expressed his views in speaking of "The Drunkard's Children," and has so delicately and yet pointedly referred to what he considered inartistic in it, that I will venture to quote the passage.

Forster says, Charles Dickens's view was that if the causes of habitual inebriation were attentively

BANK RESTRICTION- NOTE

Specimen of a Bank Note — not to be imitated.

Submitted to the Consideration of the Bank-Directors and the inspection of the Public.

Published by WILLIAM HONE, Ludgate Hill, Price (with the Bank Restriction Barometer) One Shilling.

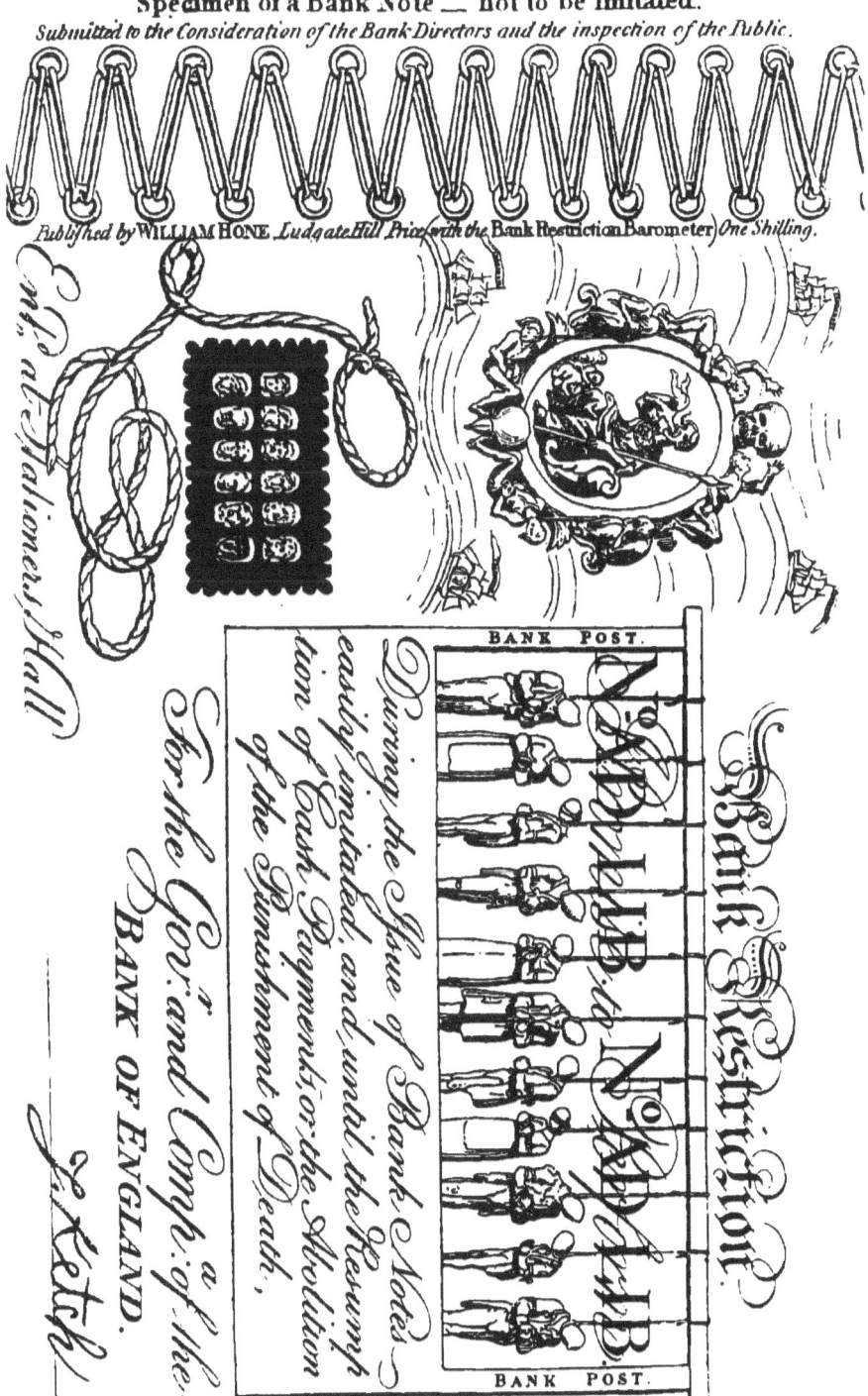

Engraved Stationers Hall

BANK POST.

Bank Restriction

N AB LL BB is N AB LL BB

During the Issue of Bank Notes easily imitated, and until the Resumption of Cash Payments, or the Abolition of the Punishment of Death,

For the Gov: and Comp: of the
BANK OF ENGLAND.

J. Ketch

BANK POST.

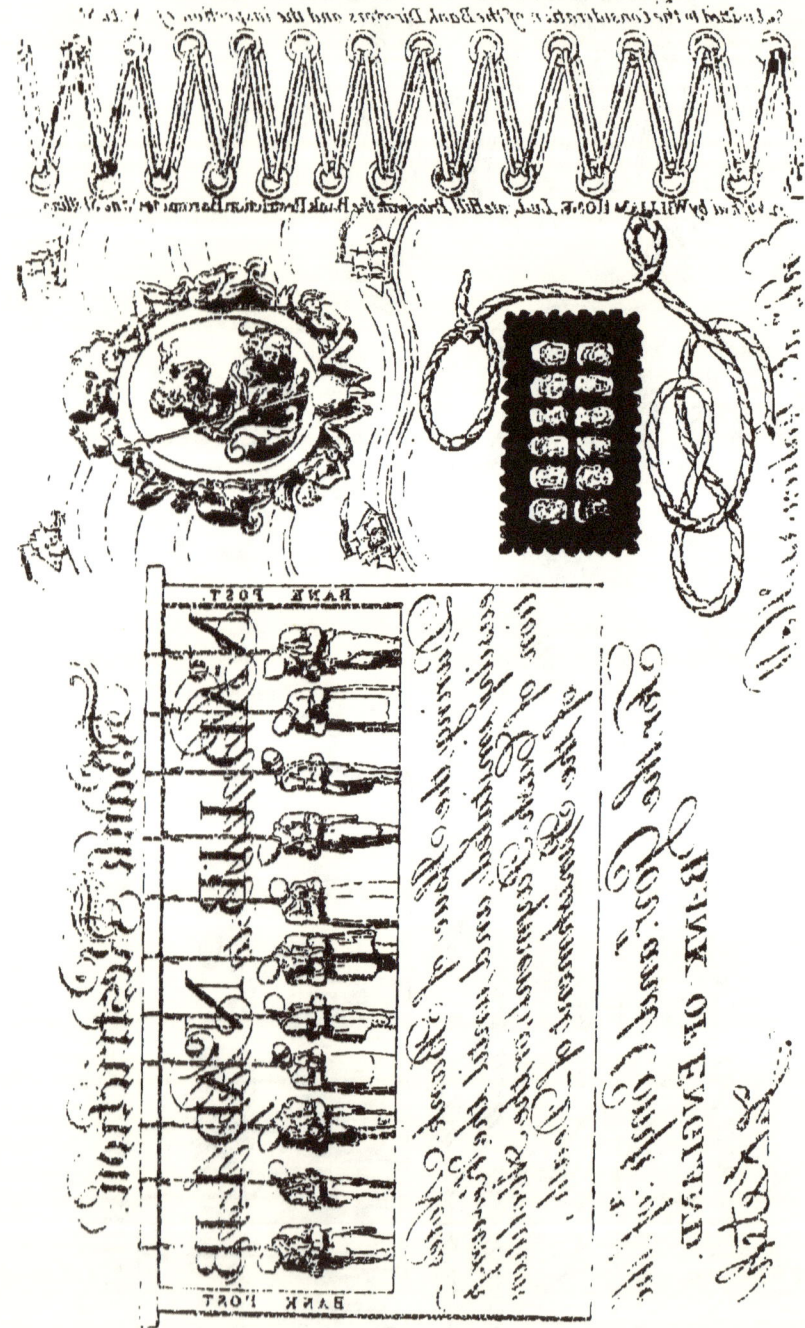

BANK RESTRICTION NOTE.

Specimen of a Bank Note.— not to be imitated.

studied, they would be found, in nine out of ten cases, to consist of the *want* of clean, wholesome dwellings, light workshops, and healthy work, plenty of light, air, and water—the want of the means, in fact, of leading decent, cleanly, and healthy lives, with a certain small share of relaxation and excitement, and the power of obtaining food for the mind as well as the body, to fill up those hours not monopolised with work, and which are now mainly spent in beer-shops.

"I think," said Charles Dickens (speaking of "The Drunkard's Children") "the power of that closing scene quite extraordinary. It haunts the remembrance like an awful reality. There are other fine things, too. The deathbed scene on board the hulks—the convict who is composing the face, and the other who is drawing the screen round the bed, seem to me masterpieces worthy of the greatest painter. In the trial scene at the Old Bailey the eye may wander round the court, and observe everything that is a part of the place; the very light and atmosphere are faithfully reproduced. So in the gin-shop and the beer-shop. An inferior hand would indicate a fragment of the fact and slur it over, but here every shred is honestly made out. But it only makes more exasperating to me the obstinate onesidedness of the thing. When a man shows so forcibly the side of the medal on which the people in their faults and crimes are stamped, he is the more bound to help us to a glance at that other side, on which the faults and vices of the Government placed over the people are not less gravely impressed."

The *Sketches by Boz* and *Oliver Twist* are the only works of Dickens which CRUIKSHANK illustrated: whatever may have been the causes why he did no more work in conjunction with the great novelist, it will always be a source of regret that the hand which created Bill Sykes and Fagin did not also give us a portrait of Pecksniff or Pickwick, Sam Weller, Mr. Micawber, or Dick Swiveller.

In *Oliver Twist* there are two exceptionally clever plates, those of Sykes and his dog in the fields after the murder, and Fagin in the condemned cell, which latter is terribly realistic.

In the above enumeration I have not included *The*

D

Life of Grimaldi, because Dickens was really only the editor of that work, which certainly few would purchase at the present time, but for the sake of obtaining CRUIKSHANK'S droll sketches of the various incidents in the life of the great clown.

Dickens and CRUIKSHANK were old friends, and, before this unfortunate Temperance misunderstanding, performed together in amateur theatricals ; in one case, Dickens played Justice Shallow, when CRUIKSHANK took Pistol. The following humourous account of the artist's personal appearance was written by Dickens thirty years ago :—

Mrs. Gamp speaks—"I do assure you, Mrs. Harris, when I stood in the railways office that morning with my bundle on one arm and one patten in my hand, you might have knocked me down with a feather, far less porkmangers which was a-lumping against me continual and severe all round. I was drove about like a brute animal, and almost worrited into fits, when a gentleman with a large shirt collar, and a hook nose, and a eye like one of Mr. Sweedlepipes's hawks, and long locks of hair, and whiskers that I wouldn't have no lady as I was engaged to meet suddenly a-turning round a corner for any sum of money you could offer me, says, laughing, 'Halloa, Mrs. Gamp, what are *you* up to?' I didn't know him from a man (except by his clothes), but I says faintly, 'If you're a Christian man, show me where to get a second-cladge ticket for Manjestir, and have me put in a carridge, or I shall drop.'"

———

CRUIKSHANK has frequently inserted portraits of himself in his drawings, and the enumeration of a few instances may be of service, as it will always be interesting to turn to the likeness of the man whose works are so celebrated.

The Table Book.—"The Triumph of Cupid," one of the most beautiful examples of the artist's power as an etcher, which is literally crowded with types of humanity, all under the spell of the naughty little god, is remarkable for containing no less than three portraits of GEORGE CRUIKSHANK. He is the central figure, seated by the fireside, calmly indulging in the luxury of a pipe, whence issues a marvellous wreath of smoke, which takes the form of the various classes of English society. The motto is—" *Ex Fumo dare Lucem.*" The details of the right-hand side of this illustration are marvellous, both in conception and execution ; the little imp astride of the artist's foot, toasting a heart at the blazing fire, whilst his muscular little brother has just " polished off " a gigantic dustman with the gloves, are not a whit inferior to the celebrated dancing elves in *Grimm's Fairy Tales.*

The Omnibus.—Article entitled " My Portrait " contains two humorous sketches of G. CRUIKSHANK. One of these, namely, "GEORGE CRUIKSHANK entering a Drawing-room," was reprinted in *Pro and Con* for March, 1873.

Ainsworth's Magazine.—" Our Library Table " contains portraits of G. CRUIKSHANK and W. H. Ainsworth, consulting together.

Sketches by Boz.—Plate, " Public Dinners." Two old gentlemen lead the way, followed by Charles Dickens on the left and GEORGE CRUIKSHANK on the right.

Many years ago there appeared in *Fraser's Magazine* a series of articles written by Dr. Maginn to illustrations by Maclise, representing various celebrated literary characters. GEORGE CRUIKSHANK was one of them, and Maginn says of the portrait :—

" Here we have the sketcher sketched ; and, as is fit, he is sketched sketching. Here is GEORGE CRUIKSHANK—the GEORGE CRUIKSHANK !—seated upon the head of a barrel, catching inspiration from the scenes presented to him in a pot-house, and consigning the ideas of the moment to immortality on the top of his hat."

That was some years before he " took the pledge." The above-named portrait was reproduced in the *Illustrated Sporting and Dramatic News* of February 9, 1878.

In the *London Journal*, November 20, 1847, a capital likeness was given, with an interesting biographical notice, and some sketches copied from the series of " The Bottle."

———

It would be giving the artist credit for enormous reading to assert that he first perused every work he illustrated, yet when it is considered how felicitous are his plates to the books, how well the best incidents are chosen for artistic portrayal, how correct all the accessories are to the context, and how carefully and completely each individual is made to retain his individuality all through the work—the fidelity of his drawing in natural scenery, architectural details, and the historical costumes of almost every age—it will be seen that only by study of a wide and extremely general character could he have arrived at such excellence in so many, and widely-varying topics.

One great merit in the works of GEORGE CRUIKSHANK is the remarkable absence of anything indelicate, far less indecent.

In a few only of the earlier sketches, drawn 50 years ago, when public taste was less fastidious than it is now, can anything at all questionable be found. And this is indeed saying a great deal for an artist who had to illustrate the works of such outspoken authors as Swift, Fielding, Smollett and Defoe.

As to the good taste of some of his early political caricatures, it is not easy now to speak positively. In the days of the despicable and detested Prince Regent, public opinion was violently opposed to his cruel and cowardly treatment of his wife; and whatever may have been that lady's faults, it is pleasant to see that GEORGE CRUIKSHANK was an ardent supporter of her claims to justice and fair treatment.

Curiously enough, he was at first inclined to side with

the Prince; indeed the English disposition seems to be to bear with the follies—even the vices—of Royalty, to a point which it is positive other modern nations would not allow in their rulers.

When, however, George the Regent was plainly seen to be nothing but a cruel, profligate wretch, without a single redeeming point, not even the *strong loyalty* of such a man as CRUIKSHANK could induce him to remain in the ranks of the followers of a prince who had violated every law of honour and morality—whose life was as false, cruel, and useless, as his death was shameful, lingering, and agonising.

It were unnecessary, even if it were possible, to add to the universal execrations which followed the corse of George IV. to his grave, but *it is* necessary to point out that CRUIKSHANK was more than justified for every line he drew in his political caricatures of the days of the Regency.

That CRUIKSHANK was loyal, and had ever been so since the death of George, every action in his life has proved; and that he was a true patriot will be gathered from the facts that he was a Volunteer when the first Napoleon was agitating Europe, and that when the Volunteer movement again revived in 1859 he joined enthusiastically in the cause, and was for some years the commanding officer of one of the largest corps in London. It must be remembered that the Havelock Volunteers, of which corps he was Lieutenant-Colonel, were all supposed to be total abstainers.

It would be doing the artist an injustice were we not to consider in what points he was sometimes at a loss, and to draw attention to what may be called faults. These are but small matters, and, considering the enormous number of his works, it is surprising how few cases there are in which it can be said that he failed to do justice to the author's conceptions, or erred in the artistic treatment of a subject. Yet it must be con-

fessed that his ideal of female beauty is not usually
happy. In this particular he is certainly inferior to
Du Maurier, who draws lovely female faces, but even
that artist seems to be limited in his stock of models,
for all his ladies have a wonderful family likeness, and
all, or nearly all, are represented as giantesses; for, if we
are to judge of the height of these ladies by their sur-
roundings, few of them will be found to stand less than
six feet high, and some are even taller than that. In
some respects the result is pleasing, the long, flowing
skirts and the graceful curves give an air of elegance
to the forms, but as the French poet so well expresses it,
" *Rien n'est beau que le vrai*," and as women are already
made lovely by nature, art might rest content to paint
them as they are—our hearts would suffer none the less.

CRUIKSHANK, too, has not been over successful in
delineating the *real* gentleman ; *snobs*, and *gents* he has
shown to the life, with their flashy jewellery, their
striped and checked and spotted clothes, their sticks,
and hats perched on one side of the head with a would-
be jaunty air. But the plain, well dressed, carefully
clean, but withal jolly, good looking, and dashing gentleman we seldom, if ever, find in CRUIKSHANK. Perhaps
this is owing to the singular changes in fashion which
have come to pass since the days when most of GEORGE
CRUIKSHANK'S pictures of social life were drawn ;
or, what is more probable, the artist found it more con-
genial to his tastes to provoke mirth by seizing upon the
ridiculous and exaggerated side of human nature rather
than to design namby-pamby groups of every-day
people, such as we now see in most of the magazines.
Such illustrations may well be more natural, and if
Lord St. John did meet Lady Flora at the garden gate,
the occurrence would probably have appeared something like it is drawn; but we never think of looking
twice at such a picture, and certainly would not pre-
serve it.

The caricatures of the ridiculous fashions of his youthful days laughed away many absurdities, and helped to bring in a more rational style of costume.

Sometimes, but not often, the scenery in CRUIK-SHANK'S plates is defective, the trees look woolly and stage-like; but once and for all let it be said, that, when his merits are considered, CRUIKSHANK will not be praised as a portrait painter, as a landscape artist, or as an illustrator of books of fashion. His genius was creative, not imitative. It is nearly forty years ago since the *Quarterly Review* (by no means enthusiastically given to praise at any time), in making mention of GEORGE CRUIKSHANK, commented on the absurdity of excluding such a man from the Royal Academy, because his works were not produced in certain materials, and did not occupy a certain space in its annual shows :—

" Will no Associates be found upon its books, one of these days, the labours of whose oil and brushes will have sunk into the profoundest obscurity, when many pencil-marks of Mr. CRUIKSHANK and of Mr. Leech will be still fresh in half the houses in the land ? "

Whilst Thackeray still more enthusiastically praises him, and pleads eloquently for love and admiration for his good and noble work :—

" He has told a thousand truths, in as many strange and fascinating ways. He has given a thousand new and pleasant thoughts to millions of people ; he has never used his wit dishonestly ; he has never, in all the exuberance of his frolicsome humour, caused a single painful or guilty blush. How little do we think of the extraordinary power of this man, and how ungrateful we are to him ! "

When Thackeray wrote, it was quite within the mark to style the British public "ungrateful;" but, thanks partly to that article, partly to the better appreciation of art which has arisen in recent years, the fame of CRUIKSHANK increased from day to day, until he came to be looked upon with something of the reverence and all the love that we generally only accord to great men after death.

Even professional art critics came at length to see that this wonderful outsider, who belonged to no school in particular, had some merit.

P. G. Hamerton says, in his *Etching and Etchers,* 1876 :—

"There is in CRUIKSHANK an artist within or behind the caricaturist; and this artist is a personage of exceptional endowment. His invention is vivid, and his power of drawing the figures invented is singularly sprightly and precise. There are etchings by CRUIK-SHANK, though these are not numerous in proportion to the mass of his great labours, which are as excellent artistically as they are notable for genius and wit, where the stroke of the needle is as happy as the thought, and where the student of etching may find models, as the student of manners finds a record, or a suggestion.

"In etchings of this class, CRUIKSHANK carries one great virtue of the art to perfection—its simple frankness. He is so direct and unaffected that only those who know the difficulties of etching can appreciate the power that lies behind his unpretending skill; there is never, in his most admirable plates, the trace of a vain effort."

It must be remembered that all the copper plates and steel etchings were entirely the work of CRUIKSHANK'S own hands ; it was only the woodcuts which he entrusted to the professional engravers.

In some of his works CRUIKSHANK has been much indebted to the wood engravers for the success of his drawings, one remarkable instance is *Three Courses and a Dessert,* in which the cuts are most charmingly executed.

An able article on wood engraving in the *London and Westminster Review,* August 1838, points out some of the most celebrated wood engravers of forty years ago. It particularly distinguishes two families, the *Thompsons* and the *Williamses,* and it may be remembered that these names are attached to many of CRUIKSHANK'S best works. A skilful and talented draughtsman is of little use as an illustrator, unless his work can be done justice to by the wood engraver.

Mr. Ruskin, in his *Modern Painters*, regrets that such marvellous powers should have been devoted to illustrating books. In this feeling it is impossible to concur; for if we can judge of posterity, it will value CRUIK-SHANK less for his oil-colour paintings, or his political caricatures, than for the wonderful talent he has displayed in giving to authors' "airy nothings a local habitation and a name."

Amongst his most celebrated oil paintings are "Disturbing a Congregation," painted for the late Prince Consort, and the "Worship of Bacchus," executed in 1863. This extraordinary work of imagination, which measures 13 feet 4 inches by 7 feet 8 inches, contains a large number of figures in various stages of inebriation, and cost the artist more than twelve months' almost incessant labour. It was purchased by the Temperance Society, by whom it was presented to the nation, and is now in the South Kensington Museum.

———

A taste for collecting old books and caricatures is a very harmless one. It affords much innocent recreation to oneself, and is a source of amusement for our friends.

But to thoroughly carry out this taste three things are necessary—money, time, and knowledge.

Hogarth, Gilray and Rowlandson's works are dear and scarce, and G. CRUIKSHANK'S are daily becoming more sought after.

Many of his early works were not signed, especially the political caricatures. Besides which his early style so much resembled the work of his father and brother as to render it difficult to decide the authorship of many old cuts.

First editions of books containing his illustrations

often sell for ten times their original value, and a few of them can no longer be met with at any price; indeed it is probable that no complete set of his works exists anywhere.

There are a few well-known collectors, and one of these gentlemen has bought up as many of the steel and copper plates and woodcuts as possible, so that no more illustrations can be printed from them. By so doing the value of the original impressions is kept up, but the outside public is thus debarred from obtaining copies of some of his best illustrations.

THE CRUIKSHANK-AINSWORTH CONTROVERSY.

By far the most important event in the latter years of CRUIKSHANK'S life was the newspaper controversy which arose between him and Mr. W. H. Ainsworth. It is unnecessary to refer at length to the writings of Mr. Ainsworth, but without a few words of explanation concerning this controversy, any notice of CRUIK-SHANK'S life would be decidedly incomplete. Concerning the novel of *Jack Sheppard*, Mr. Thackeray wrote :—

"It seems to us that Mr. Cruikshank really created the tale, and that Mr. Ainsworth, as it were, only put words to it. Let any reader of the novel think over it for awhile, let him think and tell us what he remembers of the tale. George Cruikshank's pictures— always George Cruikshank's pictures. The Storm on the Thames, for instance. All the author's laboured description of that event has passed clean away. We have only before the mind's eye the fine plates of Cruikshank: the poor wretch cowering under the bridge arch, as the waves come rushing in, and the boats are whirling away in the drift of the great swollen, black waters.

"The author requires many pages to describe the fury of the storm which Mr. Cruikshank has represented in one. And let any man look at that second plate—of the Murder on the Thames—and he must acknowledge how much more brilliant the artist's description is than the writer's, and what a real genius for the terrible, as well as for the ridiculous, the former has."

This paragraph seems to have been written in a prophetic spirit, for, as we all know, GEORGE CRUIK-SHANK really did, a few years ago, claim credit for having originated the plots of several of the novels said to have been written by W. H. Ainsworth, but what was still more startling, he put himself forward as the author of the most important parts of *Oliver Twist.*

In Forster's *Life of Dickens,* he alluded, in no very complimentary terms, to MR. CRUIKSHANK'S claim to having originated *Oliver Twist,* upon seeing which notice, the artist wrote a letter to *The Times* fully explaining the particulars. He says,—

"When *Bentley's Miscellany* was first started, it was arranged that Mr. Charles Dickens should write a serial in it, and which was to be illustrated by me ; and in a conversation with him as to what the subject should be for the first serial, I suggested to Mr. Dickens that he should write the life of a London boy, and strongly advised him to do this, assuring him that I would furnish him with the subject, and supply him with all the characters, which my large experience of London life would enable me to do.

"My idea was to raise a boy from a most humble position up to a high and respectable one—in fact, to illustrate one of those cases of common occurrence where men of humble origin, by natural ability, industry, honest and honourable conduct, raise themselves to first-class positions in society. And as I wished particularly to bring the habits and manners of the thieves of London before the public (and this for a most important purpose, which I shall explain one of these days), I suggested that the poor boy should fall among thieves, but that his honesty and natural good disposition should enable him to pass through this ordeal without contamination ; and after I had fully described the full-grown thieves (the *Bill Sykeses*) and their female companions, also the young thieves (the *Artful Dodgers*) and the receivers of stolen goods, Mr. Dickens agreed to act on my suggestion, and the work was commenced, but we differed as to what sort of boy the hero should be. Mr. Dickens wanted rather a queer kind of chap, and, although this was contrary to my original idea, I complied with his request, feeling that it would not be right to dictate too much to the writer of the story, and then appeared ' *Oliver Asking for More ;*' but it so happened just about this time that an inquiry was being made in the parish of St. James's, Westminster, as to the cause of the death of some of the workhouse children who had been ' farmed out.' I called the attention of Mr. Dickens to this inquiry, and said that if he took up this matter, his doing so might help to save many a poor child from injury and death ; and I earnestly begged of him to let me make Oliver a nice pretty little boy, and if we so represented him, the public—and particularly the ladies—would be sure to take a greater interest in him, and the work would then be a certain success. Mr. Dickens agreed to that request, and I need not add here that my prophecy was fulfilled ; and if any one will take the trouble to look at my representations of ' Oliver,' they will see that the appearance of the boy is altered after the two first illustrations, and, by a reference to the records of St. James's parish, and to the date of the publication of the *Miscellany*, they will see that both the dates tally, and therefore support my statement.

" I had, a long time previously to this, directed Mr. Dickens's attention to Field Lane, Holborn Hill, wherein resided many thieves and receivers of stolen goods, and it was suggested that one of these receivers, a Jew, should be introduced into the story ; and upon one occasion Mr. Dickens and Mr. Harrison Ainsworth called upon me, and in course of conversation I described and performed the character of one of these Jew receivers, and this was the origin of Fagin."

He then proceeds to state that nearly all his designs were made in consequence of conversations he had with Mr. Dickens, and that he never saw any of the manuscript of the novel until it was nearly finished, and it must be remembered that it came out in parts.

It can never be ascertained in such a question as this, to what extent the exchange of ideas by two men in the course of long and repeated interviews may have influenced the minds of both. It cannot be doubted for a moment that Mr. CRUIKSHANK's greater age, experience and astonishing powers of observation, must have been of immense service to Charles Dickens, then a very young man, with but a slight knowledge of London, who with his wonderful descriptive faculty clearly shows us in language the scenes which the artist has rendered so faithfully in his illustrations, and it may truly be said that *Oliver Twist* lives as much in our memory through CRUIKSHANK as through Dickens.

The same remark certainly does not apply to the set of novels written by W. Harrison Ainsworth, and illustrated by CRUIKSHANK, for, but for the illustrations, such books as *Jack Sheppard, Guy Fawkes, The Tower of London*, and *The Miser's Daughter* would have long since been forgotten, nor do they deserve a better fate.

How immeasurably superior the plates are in these works to the letterpress, anyone can judge, and Thackeray's opinion has already been given on that point. Yet when Andrew Halliday, in 1872, dramatised *The Miser's Daughter*, and all the best scenic effects were modelled directly in imitation of CRUIKSHANK'S plates, not a word was said about him, and the public were led to suppose that the credit of the piece rested with Mr. Ainsworth, from whom Mr. Halliday had permission to dramatise the novel. Naturally resenting such treatment, CRUIKSHANK wrote to *The Times*, and fully explained the large share he had in the construction and plot, not only of *The Miser's Daughter*, but also of *The Tower of London*.

No one who is well acquainted with the marvellous works of this artist will consider that had he been the author of any or all of the Ainsworth novels his fame would have been thereby enhanced one iota; but such was his character for strict veracity, that no person can doubt for one moment that his account of the origin of these novels is perfectly accurate, and in justice to him, I take leave to repeat the substance of the explanations contained in his little pamphlet, entitled, *The Artist and the Author*, published by Bell and Daldy. Referring, in the first place, to *The Miser's Daughter*, he states :—

"My idea, suggested to Mr. Ainsworth, was to write a story in which the principal character should be a miser, who had a daughter, and that the struggles of feeling between the love for his child and his love of money, should produce certain effects and results; and as all my ancestors were nursed up in the Rebellion of

'45, I suggested that the story should be of that date, in order that I might introduce some scenes and circumstances connected with that great party struggle, and also wishing to let the public of the present day, have a peep at the places of public amusement of that period. I took considerable pains to give correct views and descriptions of those places which are now copied and produced upon the stage (at the Adelphi Theatre), and I take this opportunity of complimenting my friend Halliday for the very excellent and effective manner in which he has dramatised the story.

"I do not mean to say that Mr. Ainsworth, when writing this novel, did not introduce some of his own ideas; but as the first idea, and all the principal points and characters emanated from me, I think it will be allowed that the title of *originator* of *The Miser's Daughter* should be mine."

He then enumerates the following works, and explains what share he had in their production :—*Rookwood, Jack Sheppard, Guy Fawkes, The Tower of London, Old St. Paul's, The Miser's Daughter, Windsor Castle, St. James's—or the Court of Queen Anne.*

"Six of these works (he says) were illustrated entirely by me, and one, *Windsor Castle*, partly so, numbering altogether 144 of the very best designs and etchings I have ever produced.

"*Rookwood* (which is the history of Dick Turpin, the highwayman) was written and published before I became acquainted with Mr. Ainsworth, but I illustrated for him what was, I believe, a second or third edition of this work.

"*Jack Sheppard*. Illustrated by me and published in monthly parts in *Bentley's Miscellany*. This story originated from Mr. Ainsworth, and when preparing it for publication, he showed me about two or three pages of manuscript on post paper, and *I beg that it may be observed that this was the only bit of manuscript written by this author that I ever saw in the whole course of my life.*

"*Guy Fawkes*. Suggested by Mr. Ainsworth and illustrated by me, and published in *Bentley's Miscellany*.

"*The Tower of London*. The original idea of which was suggested by me to Mr. Ainsworth, and also illustrated by me, was published in monthly numbers. In this work Mr. Ainsworth and I were *partners*, holding equal shares.

"*Old St. Paul's*. This was illustrated by Mr. Franklin.

"*The Miser's Daughter*, already alluded to.

" *Windsor Castle*. The first part illustrated by the French artist Tony Johannot, and the remainder by me.

" *St. James's, or the Court of Queen Anne*. The last work of Mr. Ainsworth's I ever illustrated."

Having suggested the subject of *The Tower of London* to include some incidents in the life of Lady Jane Grey, Mr. CRUIKSHANK mentions that he went with Mr. Ainsworth to the Tower, and pointed out the various localities he desired to depict in his illustrations. He proceeds :—

" I have now most distinctly to state that Mr. Ainsworth *wrote up to most of my suggestions and designs*, although some of the subjects we *jointly* arranged to introduce into the work ; and I used every month to send him the *tracings* or *outlines* of the *sketches* or drawings from which I was making the etchings to illustrate the work, *in order that he might write up to them*, and that they should be *accurately described*.

" And I beg the reader to understand that all these *etchings* or *plates* were printed and ready for publication before the letterpress was printed, and sometimes even before the author had written his manuscript ; and I assert that I never saw a page of this work until after it was published, and then hardly ever read a line of it.

" It is a curious coincidence, which clearly proves what I have just stated with respect to these *outlines*, that Mr. Ainsworth, in January last, was applied to for *these* and other tracings or *outlines*, and his reply was that ' he would be very happy to send the tracings mentioned, but he had no idea what had become of them, as he had not seen them since *The Tower of London* was published.' This letter I have in my possession. When this work was completed, I told Mr. Ainsworth that I had another subject for our next work, namely, *The Plague* and the *Fire of London*.

But it seems that Mr. Ainsworth incorporated this idea in his next work—namely, *Old St. Paul's*—without employing Mr. CRUIKSHANK to illustrate it, or allowing him any share of the proceeds, after it had been distinctly understood between them that it was to be a joint undertaking. This breach of faith led, of course, to a coolness between the artist and the author, which, however, was dispelled by the exertions of

Dr. Pettigrew, and Mr. Ainsworth being then about to start a Magazine, found it advisable to renew his connection with the most popular and most gifted artist of the day.

Before *Ainsworth's Magazine* was published, advertisements were put forth that it was to be illustrated by CRUIKSHANK, and then it was, he states, that he suggested the tale of the *Miser's Daughter*. This Mr. Ainsworth adopted, and it appeared as the leading novel in his Magazine.

That was followed by *Windsor Castle* and *St. James's*, after which, Mr. Ainsworth sold the Magazine to his publishers. That Mr. Ainsworth, at that period, certainly considered CRUIKSHANK as something more than a mere illustrator of the Magazine may be judged of by reference to a small woodcut, drawn expressly for it at his request, representing the author and the artist seated in council, with their sketches, manuscripts and books scattered around them.

This cut, entitled "Our Library Table," is also interesting, as the portraits of both gentlemen are very clear and distinct, though small.

Besides which, in June, 1842, Mr. Ainsworth also published two verses, consisting of acrostics on his own name and that of Mr. CRUIKSHANK. These verses have no intrinsic merit, but they serve to show that the public considered the two gentlemen as co-partners in the work, that Mr. Ainsworth accepted that construction, and had no objection to admit Mr. CRUIKSHANK'S merits, so long as the name and genius of that gentleman were inducing the public to support *Ainsworth's Magazine.*

LITERARY ACROSTICS.

I.

WILLIAM HARRISON AINSWORTH.

When I again shall view the ancient Tower,
In living mirror of the Thames reflected ;
Looming St. Paul's (embodied art and power) ;
Learned Gray's Inn ; old Guildhall, cit respected ;
Idle Saint James's ; Windsor's royal bower—
And all those scenes with former hours connected.
Many a new creation shall I find
Hovering around the phantoms of thy mind!

AINSWORTH ! it may be that for me no more
Remembrances again shall turn to life,
Retiring while realities restore
In form and sense the sights in memory rife ;
So be it—so those scenes beheld of yore,
Of aspect dim, shall aid me in the strife—
No strife unpleasing—in due scene to assign
All those rare actions of that page of thine.

I know thee not—have seen thee not ; thy mind,
Nevertheless, breathes near me in thy line,
Shadowing thy smile or tear for human kind
When hope is crown'd or love left to repine ;
On thee the intent eye of the world I find,
Right well with that thy image I divine,
The author, thus even as his page shall be
Heart imaged—stored in the mind's treasury.

E.

II.

GEORGE CRUIKSHANK.

GEORGE CRUIKSHANK—every heart, both young and old—
Even the middle, most uncertain, aged,
Owns satisfaction as thy name is told;
Renown'd for long successful battle waged
'Gainst devils blue, that so in thraldom hold
English hearts, ever by themselves encaged.
CRUIKSHANK! I do rejoice to see thy name
Reckon'd with Ainsworth's in the roll of fame!

Union most pregnant! that with grace doth bind
In faithful bonds such pencil and such pen—
Kith bound to kin, and neither less than kind;
So shall *young graces* bless us now and then.
Heaven marries truly such a mind and mind,
And shall command for both the hopes of men.
Now, trustful, let us forth with thee and Ainsworth,
Knowing full well it will be worth the pain's worth.

V.V., D.D.

After Mr. Ainsworth sold his Magazine to the publishers, Mr. CRUIKSHANK never again illustrated that author's works, and it is scarcely necessary here to say that beyond those that are so illustrated, the public know very little of Mr. Ainsworth's writings, which are slowly sinking into oblivion, and will be well nigh forgotten in fifty years' time. On the point at issue Mr. CRUIKSHANK ably pointed out in what his work differed from that of an ordinary magazine illustrator:—

" The ordinary way (he states) is for the author to write out *from his own ideas* the whole of the tale, or in parts; the manuscript or letterpress is then handed to the artist to *read* and *select* subjects from for his illustrations, or sometimes the author suggests such parts or scenes as he might wish to be illustrated. But I will now explain that *Oliver Twist, The Tower of London*, and *The Miser's Daughter* were produced in an entirely different manner from what would be considered the usual course; for *I suggested to the authors of these works the original idea or subject* for them to write out, furnishing at the same time *the principal characters and scenes*, and then, as the tale had to be produced in monthly parts, the writer and the artist had every month to settle what subjects were to be introduced; and the author had to weave in such scenes as I wished to represent, and sometimes I had to work out his suggestions."

Mr. CRUIKSHANK's statement is so clear and explicit, and his honour and integrity so undoubted, that posterity will, doubtless, give him credit for that share in the authorship of these books which he claimed. It will do so with the more certainty, as the only person capable of modifying or qualifying Mr. CRUIKSHANK's statements—namely, Mr. Ainsworth—contented himself with writing the following brief and not over courteous letter to the *Times*:—

"SIR,—I disdain to reply to Mr. Cruikshank's preposterous assertions, except to give them a flat contradiction.
"Your faithful servant,
"W. HARRISON AINSWORTH.
"*April* 11*th*, 1872."

To style the circumstantial narrative of the great artist "*preposterous assertions*," and to flatly contradict a statement *in toto*, of which some parts *must necessarily be, and obviously are, true*, is a mode of replying to an adversary—either in an argument or in a law court—which damages the person who uses it far more than the person against whom it is directed.

BIBLIOGRAPHICAL NOTES.

Dr, Syntax's Life of Napoleon, in Hudibrastic verse, with coloured illustrations by G. C., published by W. Tegg in 1815. This work is now very scarce, there not being a copy even in the British Museum library.

Peter Schlemihl. The first edition of this remarkable work, published by Whittaker, in 1824, has an error on the title, a second " c " being inserted in the name " Cruickshank " ; this was altered after a few copies had been printed.

Impressions with the extra " c " are scarce, and being indisputably early copies fetch a high price.

Italian Tales, 1824. Sixteen illustrations. The first edition of this work contains a cut, facing page 58, representing a monk at his devotions, and another monk throwing a stone at him. This cut was suppressed in later editions for reasons which anyone who has seen the illustration will readily understand.

In *Hone's Every Day Book,* August 25th, 1827, there is a kindly notice of *Phrenological Illustrations,* then newly published, concluding with the advice to town purchasers that it would be a well-timed compliment to Mr. CRUIKSHANK if they were to direct their steps to his house, No. 25, Myddleton Terrace, Pentonville. The same work has a few signed drawings by CRUIKSHANK, the best of which are " The Barrow Woman," The Fantocini," "Gymnastics," and "Guy Fawkes." It is well-known that he contributed many other drawings to Mr. Hone, but unfortunately his signature is not appended to them.

This humourous cut is one of seven designs furnished
by GEORGE CRUIKSHANK to illustrate a curious little
pamphlet on Catholic Miracles, which was published by
Knight and Lacey in 1825, and is now exceedingly

scarce. It represents a band of sacrilegious robbers,
who, having broken into a monastery, proceed out of
bravado to ring a peal of bells, when, by the prayers of
the holy fathers, a miracle is wrought, and the robbers
are unable to leave their hold on the ropes.

The Young Lady's Book. London, 1829. Contains
only one plate by GEORGE CRUIKSHANK, and that is
unsigned. It is, however, quite unmistakable, being the
representation of an archery meeting, facing page 419.

" Dr. Dodd's sermon on Malt "—a quaint sketch from an old pamphlet.

" The Fantocini " is somewhat similar to a cut by GEORGE CRUIKSHANK in *Hone's Every-Day Book*, page 1114.

The Loving Ballad of Lord Bateman, originally published in 1839, has been frequently reprinted. It is
deservedly popular, both on account of the clever
etchings and Charles Dickens's humorous notes.

The history of this little work is that CRUIKSHANK
sang the old English ballad of *Lord Bateman* at a
dinner of the Antiquarian Society, with the Cockney
mal-pronunciations he had heard given to it by a street
ballad singer. Dickens and Thackeray were present,
and the latter said, " I should like to print that ballad
with illustrations ; " but, as CRUIKSHANK intimated
that he was going to do the same thing, Thackeray grace-
fully retired from the field. The original ballad is much
longer than Mr. CRUIKSHANK'S version, and has not the
slightest resemblance to a comic song. The air was
made popular a few years ago by Mr. Sothern's intro-
duction of it into *The Wild Goose Chase*, then being
played at the Haymarket Theatre.

Amongst the best of CRUIKSHANK'S fairy illustrations
are those in the *Pentamerone*. This curious collection
of tales was translated from the Neapolitan of Giam-
battista Basile by J. E. Taylor, in 1848, and published

by David Bogue, with six fine steel engravings. In his preface the translator remarks :—

" The *Pentamerone* contains fifty stories, of which I have given thirty. The gross license in which Basile allowed his humour to indulge is wholly inadmissible at the present day in a work intended for the general reader. At the same time it must be remembered that such offensive license in style and language did not convey to the Neapolitan in the seventeenth century, the same degree of coarseness that it does to our ears, simply because he connected with it very different ideas of propriety."

Consequently there exists no complete printed English translation of the *Pentamerone ;* but some years ago, the well-known bibliophile, M. Delepierre, handed the author the unpublished tales in French, with instructions to translate them for the press. It was found, however, that they were really unfit for publication, owing to their gross *indelicacy*. This is the more to be regretted, as they contain a wonderful store of poetical imagery, and for the student of proverbial philosophy, would be full of interest.

It is well known that Mr. Truman, of Bond Street, is a great collector of Cruikshankiana, and it is generally supposed that he has the original plates used for *Grimm's Fairy Tales*, as well as many others, so that many of these works can never be re-issued with the illustrations, except by means of copies. The late Mr. Hotten, of Piccadilly, pursued the latter course, when, in 1875, he republished the *German Popular Stories*, with the twenty-two wonderful etchings, *after* the original illustrations. So excellent are these copies, that even the artist himself was deceived by them, until he discovered, by the use of his magnifying glass, that some of the features were imperfect, and the hands had not their proper complement of fingers. But, to the ordinary observer, these illustrations convey all the humour that is to be found in the originals, which are now excessively rare and costly. He who can look at

these masterpieces of etching without laughing, must,
indeed, be of a sour or dyspeptic turn. Even John
Ruskin, not usually given to praise humorous com-
positions, says :—

" These are of quite sterling and admirable art, in a class pre-
cisely parallel in elevation to the character of the tales which they
illustrate, and the original etchings were unrivalled in masterfulness
of touch since Rembrandt—in some qualities of delineation, unrivalled even by him. The copies have been so carefully executed
that at first I was deceived by them, and supposed them to be late
impressions from the plates ; and what is more, I believe the master
himself was deceived by them, and supposed them to be his own."

On the Continent these etchings are well known and
much admired; copies were made in Germany, and a
Frenchman named Ambrose Tardieu copied the first
twelve, and published them in a small volume *as his
own productions.* The title he gave was *Vieux Contes
pour l'Amusement des Grands et des Petits Enfans, ornés
de 12 gravures Comiques.* Paris, A. Boulland. 1830.

The Table Book.—The gem of *The Table Book* was an
etched microcosm, in which hundreds of tiny groups are
evolved from the fumes of G. C.'s pipe. The artist's
portrait of himself, meerschaum in mouth, with a little
King Charles on his knee, is a charming study, and
establishes the fact that at one period of his life CRUIK-
SHANK was a smoker. In later years, however, he
was as resolute in his denunciation of the weed as of
the maddening wine-cup. Only to a few very dearly
prized friends he would show himself tolerant in the
matter of tobacco. " I want you to give up drinking
and smoking," he would say, " and you tell me that if
you don't smoke you can't write. Now, I'll meet you
half way. Give up the drink, and you may smoke—
just a little."

The Journal of the Plague Year. By Daniel Defoe.
Four illustrations to this work, by GEORGE CRUIKSHANK,
are remarkable from being quite dissimilar to his usual
work, they are very artistic and highly finished.

In the preface to *Three Courses and a Dessert*, the author (Mr. Clark) hopes that the feast of reason he places before his guests will prove an agreeable repast, and that even if the *dishes* be disliked, the *plates* at least will please; but he feels bound to state that whatever faults the decorations may be chargeable with, on the score of invention, he alone is to blame, and not Mr. GEORGE CRUIKSHANK, to whom he is deeply indebted for having embellished his rude sketches in their transfer to wood, and translated them into a proper pictorial state, to make their appearance in public. They have necessarily acquired a value which they did not intrinsically possess in passing through the hands of that distinguished artist, of whom it may truly, and on this occasion especially, be said *Quod tetigit, ornavit.*

Amongst the separate etchings there are some to which every collector attaches especial value, and the following are remarable amongst them from the astonishing variety of figures, and the minute detail they contain :—

"The Opening of the Great Exhibition of 1851."

"Passing Events ; or the Tail of the Comet of 1853."

The following is a list of some of the publications containing notices of the works of GEORGE CRUIK-SHANK prior to his death :—

The Westminster Review.—No. 66. June, 1840. This contains the celebrated article by W. M. Thackeray, with many illustrations. The article has been reprinted in the recent editions of Thackeray's works, but without the illustrations.

The London Journal.—November 20, 1847. Portrait and illustrations.

Household Words. "Frauds on the Fairies." No. 184.—October 1, 1853.

Blackwood's Magazine.—August, 1863.

A Descriptive Catalogue of the Works of George Cruikshank, compiled by G. W. Reid.—1871.

✓ *The Illustrated Review.*—No. 30. January 1, 1872. Portrait and illustrations.

✓ *The Artist and the Author.*—Bell and Daldy. 1872. (A Pamphlet written by GEORGE CRUIKSHANK.)

✓ *Pro and Con.*—March, April, and May, 1873 Portrait and illustrations.

✓ *The Leisure Hour.*—November, 1875.

✓ The Christmas Number of *The Bookseller.*—1875.

✓ *The West Middlesex Advertiser.*—January 19, 1878.

In personal appearance CRUIKSHANK was slightly below the middle height, spare but solid of frame, somewhat long-armed and short-legged—as long-lived men are apt to be--and very broad in the chest. His head was massive and well shaped. He had a high forehead, blue-grey eyes, full of a cheerful, sparkling light, penthouse brows, somewhat high cheek-bones, a prominent aquiline nose, and a mouth cut in firm, sharp lines, and from whose corners grew an ambiguous pair of ornaments, which were neither moustaches, nor whiskers, nor beard, but partook vaguely of the characteristics of all three.

The portrait which faces this work is copied from one which appeared about forty-five years ago, and none of the likenesses published of late give such a truthful representation of the keen outlook, beaming with genius and good humour, which characterised him to the last.

He never realised, probably, at the time when he was producing his best work anything like the profits which are now easily gathered in by men whom posterity will not think of naming in comparison with him. He was never offered the distinction of the Royal Academy; he was never adorned with any complimentary titles or honorary degrees. His reputation was purely popular, and it had won an impregnable position among the people long before the critics ventured to recognise so much as its existence.

It is something remarkable that a satirist who chastised fashionable and popular vice for more than sixty years, almost without intermission, should have left not one drawing behind him that might not be handed round in the family circle of any English household. In this respect, at least, CRUIKSHANK might claim to be superior to Hogarth, and his inferiority in other respects is not so signal that they may not be named together as the two greatest caricaturists that England has produced.

From time to time he published little pamphlets on subjects of public welfare, exposing various follies and vices of the day. Such were *The Betting Book*, *A Discovery concerning Ghosts*, *Stop Thief!* and a *Pop-gun fired off by G. Ck.*, *in defence of the British Volunteers*.

These productions are written in a homely forcible manner, with numerous italicised passages, and resemble nothing so much as the worthy old gentleman's dramatic style of conversation.

As an actor, indeed, he would have certainly acquired a leading position, his strongly-marked expressive features over which he had a wonderful command, his mimetic skill, and his great grasp of character eminently fitted him for that profession, which he at one time seriously thought of adopting.

Immediately upon his decease being made known, the London newspapers hastened to give expression to the grief felt at the national loss, and, without exception, praised him for his noble artistic career, and his upright, useful, and virtuous private life. On the second of February, the *Times* devoted a leading article to his memory ; and, on the same day, a lengthy memoir appeared in the *Daily Telegraph*. Judging from internal evidence, the latter composition, admirable as a sketch of character, and full of kindly feeling, must have emanated from the pen of the artist's old friend and admirer, G. A. Sala. Such a pen on such a topic must needs be well worth study. The *Daily News*, also, had a short but graphic description of his life and works, and the *Standard* reviewed his career in an article, on the 4th February.

On the 9th of February the remains of GEORGE CRUIKSHANK were interred at Kensal Green Cemetery. In the cemetery several thousand ladies and gentlemen were waiting to pay the last tribute of respect to the deceased artist, and nearly every well-known face of the literary and artistic world was present. Shortly after two o'clock the funeral procession arrived at the mortuary chapel, where it was met by the Rev. Charles Stewart, M.A., who began immediately to recite the order for the burial of the dead. The coffin, which was of polished oak, was then borne into the chapel on the shoulders of four volunteers, who had formerly served in the regiment of which deceased was colonel. On the coffin plate was the simple record :—
" GEORGE CRUIKSHANK, Artist, born September 27, 1792, died February 1, 1878, aged 85." A newly-made grave, near those of Thackeray and Mdlle. Tietjens, is for the present the resting-place of the genial and kind-

hearted artist; but there are hopes that CRUIKSHANK may yet find a tomb within St. Paul's Cathedral. The Dean, on being applied to by a deputation, stated that he would most willingly have complied with their request, as he considered GEORGE CRUIKSHANK had done great good in his lifetime. At present, however, there was absolutely no room for another interment until the alterations in the crypt were completed. If at any future time there should still be a wish to remove the remains to St. Paul's, he would at once sanction this transfer.

www.ingramcontent.com/pod-product-compliance
Lightning Source LLC
Chambersburg PA
CBHW031241260626
47169CB00007B/2405